RUNAWAY ALIEN

AMAZON BEST SELLER
CHILDREN'S SCIENCE FICTION

Here's what some of our readers are saying about Runaway Alien:

"Runaway Alien is exciting, suspenseful, humorous, and educational - my kids beg me to read more! You can't go wrong with this one - Excellent!!!"

"Its great SF fun with a touch of goofy kid stuff and charming characters that force you to like them."

"My grandchildren are loving it. And frankly, so is the kid inside me."

"Funny, witty and smart read! My son won't put the book down!"

RUNAWAY

ALIEN

RUNAWAY ALIEN:

A SCIENCE FICTION ADVENTURE FOR KIDS

Alec Eberts

Paul Smith-Goodson

ISBN-13: 978-1469950006

ISBN-10: 1469950006

www.runawayalien.com

Printed in U.S.A.

First Printing January 2012

About Our Cover

Since our book is about an alien from another world, we thought it fitting that our cover had a strong tie to outer space.

The boy sitting on earth was taken from an illustration called "Reach for the Stars," which was created by Gilles Tran and Jaime Vives Piqueres. The image was rendered by astronaut Mark Shuttleworth on the International Space Station, April 25 - May 5, 2002, while he was orbiting around the earth going more than 17,000 miles per hour. This project was commissioned by Chris Cason, coordinator of the POV-Ray Development Team.

You can read about the story of its creation - how it came to happen, and what inspired it at http://www.oyonale.com/iss. Our use of this image is licensed under the Creative Commons Attribution 2.5 Generic license.

Chapter 1

The Runaway

RDex was jolted out of deep-space hibernation by a shrill and intense alarm.

At first he thought it was the pilot-in-a-chip notifying him that the starship had landed, but as his brain-circuits ramped to full power, he realized that the critical alarm – which just happened to be the most important alarm in the entire star ship -- was going berserk.

The starship had been plagued with problems since he had left home; RDex wished he had never stolen the ship. If he had to steal one, he should have stolen a newer ship that wasn't old and stupid like this one. The ship's pilot chip was so ancient that it didn't even realize a kid was flying it.

To make matters worse, the alarm had sent the elderly pilot-in-a-chip spiraling into a massive circuit seizure. RDex couldn't get a clear assessment of the problem because the crazy chip was busy chattering away in the background, mumbling about weather on the home planet while simultaneously singing a weird data tune that RDex had never heard before.

He finally managed to calm the chip down enough so he could retrieve three key scanner readings to triangulate the problem. Oh, great galaxy, he thought, it was a major failure in the navigational system.

With a failure like that, he could thank his lucky nova to have made it to the correct planet, but he needed a sane system to land the ship at the correct location. If the pilot chip didn't fully recover, it was possible that he might miss his landing zone by hundreds, or even thousands of miles.

The ship shuddered as the side thrusters fired in preparation for his descent through the planet's oxygen-rich atmosphere. Through the window on his right, the planet's moon looked impossibly huge and gloriously bright. It hung in the dark sky like an exploding star. Compared to this lunar monster, the two small moons that orbited his home planet were drab and featureless.

Atmospheric friction was increasing the outside surface temperature. The hull of the star ship would soon heat up to the point that an alien observer on the planet below would see the ship as a thin comet-like streak in the night sky. RDex stared down at the twinkling lights far below his ship and wondered if any strange beings might be looking up at him as he looked down at them.

There was always a chance -- although a very small one -- that his Primary Guide, who had been sent on a mission to gather information about this planet a few years ago, might chance a glimpse at his glowing ship arcing across the night sky. If she saw it, she would be able to recognize the signature of its blue power thruster, and know that someone had come to save her.

He missed his guide, but more than that, he was

worried about her. They had received one and only one communication from her since she had arrived on the planet. RDex was afraid that something terrible had happened to her. Perhaps she had been captured, or worse, dismantled. Concern for her well being had bolstered his courage enough to run away from home in a stolen ship. Of course, he felt guilty about stealing the ship, and he knew it had been terribly wrong. If he made it back home with her, it would be well worth it, even if he had to spend a few hundred years in penalty hibernation. His Primary Guide -- if she were still functioning -- would be angry with him, but he hoped she would also be glad to see him.

As the blue planet grew larger in the ship's viewing screen, RDex activated the landing module, punched in the landing coordinates where his Primary Guide had last reported.

He hoped he didn't end up as a pile of charred metal on a strange planet where no one had the knowledge or skill to reassemble him.

Chapter 2

The School Project

Hawk woke up with two large brown eyes staring at him and bright rays of morning sunlight slanting through the two square windows above his bed. He'd had a nightmare that he'd been drowning in a bowl of Jell-O. As the nightmarish fog cleared from his brain, he realized that his entire face was wet. He put a finger to his cheek.

Dog spit. Bug Dog had been licking his face again.

Hawk wiped his face with a corner of his pillow. "Yuk! Get off the bed Bug Dog."

Bug Dog hopped off the bed and stood beside the bed happily wagging his tail. Bug Dog was a small black pug that had never met a face he didn't like to lick. He had a curly tail and a face that looked like it had smashed into a wall going full speed.

Hawk squinted through one eye at the blue rocket clock on his bedside stand. It was seven AM and time to get started.

He was glad it was Friday. He loved Fridays, but today was extra special. There was no school because the teachers were having an all day meeting downtown. That meant no stinky bus ride, no sweaty gym class, no tests, and no yucky cafeteria food. Instead, he was going to Creepy Woods in a few hours with his best friend, Tommy.

Life was great.

Hawk dressed quickly, put on a pair of old jeans with holes in both knees, a green camouflage T-shirt purchased for scout camp last year, and black leather boots that he hadn't worn since the fifth grade. The boots were a little too short and pinched his feet. He wanted to wear them to Creepy Woods in case he stepped into a bunch of dangerous snakes. Hawk's dad had told him there weren't any poisonous snakes in their state. But Hawk had also heard his dad say at least a million times that there was a first time for everything. And being attacked by snakes definitely qualified as a first.

Hawk started downstairs for breakfast, and then stopped. He wriggled his right foot and felt a lump inside his boot.

Sock Booger!

Sock boogers were clumps of thread that lurked in the toes of his socks. Hawk had been collecting sock boogers since the second grade. He estimated that the glass jar on his dresser was stuffed with at least a million sock boogers. When he first discovered them in the second grade, he had asked his teacher, Mrs. Pilcher, if kids would read about him in history books along with the other great inventors. She said, "When it comes to sock boogers, anything is possible."

Hawk sat down on the carpet, took off his boot, and sock, and then turned the sock inside out. Stuck in the toe was a very large sock booger. It had a few pieces of colored threads mixed in with the white ones. Most sock boogers were white. He studied the new specimen with his magnifying glass

for a few minutes then put it in his collection jar.
Later, if he needed money for something special, he
figured he might be able to sell it on eBay for a lot of
money.

His dad had helped him setup an eBay account
last year. Using the account name of Hawkeye-
trader-007, he had sold a few rocks from his
collection then donated the money to a children's
charity that his school was sponsoring.

He insisted on having "Hawk" in his account
name, even though it wasn't his real name. He
actually had four names: Henry Alexander
Woodson Kraft. His friends called him Hawk
because his initials were H-A-W-K. His seventh
grade teacher, Miss Birdie, called him Hawk, but the
school principal, Mrs. Dorkmeyer, called him Henry.

Mrs. Dorkmeyer didn't like him. Probably
because of last year's "Squirrel Incident," as Mrs.
Dorkmeyer called it. She had misunderstood a
sincere effort on his part to further his scientific
knowledge. He had been walking to school with
Tommy when they found a dead squirrel on the

sidewalk. His science class was studying small animal skeletons so finding a dead squirrel on that particular day seemed like fate had put it there for him to find. Hawk wrapped the dead squirrel in a plastic bag so it didn't leak, and then stored the bag in his gym locker so he would remember to take it to science class.

Unfortunately, he forgot about the squirrel, so it lay in his gym locker over a very hot three day June weekend. It wasn't his fault that the school engineer had picked that particular weekend to turn off the air-conditioning for maintenance.

When everyone returned the following Monday, the school was filled with the sickly-sweet odor of decaying squirrel. Mrs. Dorkmeyer was forced to close the school for two extra days so the local HAZMAT team could clean it up. The evening news featured Mrs. Dorkmeyer looking frazzled, wearing a paper mask and rubber gloves. A HAZMAT guy, who was trying to be helpful, appeared at Mrs. Dorkmeyer's side and held up the dead squirrel for the viewing audience to see. One whiff of the odorous carcass being held by its tail in front of her face was enough to send Mrs. Dorkmeyer running in the opposite direction.

As thanks for having their vacation extended by two additional days, Hawk's class held a special election and voted him honorary class president. Everything considered, Hawk thought it turned out to be a good day for everyone.

Downstairs, Hawk's dad was sitting at the kitchen table drinking coffee and reading the news on his laptop computer. Benny, his three-year old brother, was squirming in his booster chair and finger painting in a pool of Nutty Crunchy Oats cereal he had dumped on the table.

His sister Wanda, who was in the tenth grade and had to go to school, was in the bathroom. On school days, she stayed the bathroom for hours so she could put on her makeup, get dressed, and stare at herself in the mirror. When Wanda had a sleepover two weeks ago, Hawk had walked into Wanda's bedroom to ask her a question, and all four girls were lined up in front of the mirror, staring at their reflections, both front and back. Hawk had no idea why girls did that. His dad, who claimed to be an expert on females, had once told Hawk to come to him with any questions he might have about girls, but when Hawk asked him why girls stared at themselves, he said he had no idea, and told Hawk to ask to his mother.

"You're late for school," Hawk's dad said, without looking up from his computer.

Hawk took a seat at the table. "Tommy is coming over this morning and we're riding our bikes to Creepy Woods to hunt animal tracks for Miss Birdies nature assignment. Did you forget there's no school today?"

His dad grunted, which either meant yes or no.

Creepy Woods was probably the best place in the world to look for animal tracks, and it was only a few miles from his house.

Hawk's mom placed a bowl of her "secret breakfast special" in front of him and gave him a kiss on the cheek. "Good morning, sweetie," she said.

Hawk had given his mom permission to call him 'sweetie' in the house, but nowhere else.

Her secret breakfast special wasn't really secret and it wasn't really special. It was only oatmeal with blue food coloring in it. Hawk pretended not to know because he didn't want to hurt her feelings.

"Mmmm. Great, mom," he said wolfing down a spoonful of the not-really-special special.

"Why, thank you, dear," she said, smiling.

Hawk's dad finally looked up from his computer. "What did you think about the comet we saw last night?"

"Meteorite," Hawk said.

"Huh?"

"It was a meteorite, dad," Hawk corrected. "And, I thought it was really cool."

His dad grunted, and looked back at the laptop.

Hawk stayed up late last night with his dad to look at the moon through his telescope. They had seen a large meteorite streak across the sky. Later, they watched a special news report about the sighting. One of the reporters had made a video of the meteorite, which he played over and over during his report. A bearded professor from the local college drew a diagram of the meteorite's path across the sky and speculated that it had come from a star outside the solar system. A second professor, who was short and bald, disagreed with the first professor's theory and explained in detail why he was completely wrong. After a short argument, they got into a fight. Hawk wanted to see how the fight ended, but the TV station went to a quick commercial. When the news program came back on, both professors were gone.

Hawk never knew meteorites could be so exciting.

"It was probably just a plane," Hawk's mom said, putting bowls into the dishwasher. "You know how those reporters are. They always try to make things sound more exciting than they really are."

His dad nodded.

After breakfast, Hawk took out the trash, and then fed Bug Dog. Just as he was getting his backpack out of the closet, the doorbell rang. It was Tommy. His backpack looked really full, like they were going for a week, instead of just an hour or two. Hawk knew it was probably stuffed with potato chips, candy bars, and other snacks. He saw the end of Tommy's trumpet sticking out of his pack.

Tommy could puff out his cheeks bigger than any kid in the school. Tommy said it was good training for the trumpet. He wanted to be the best trumpet player in the world, but the only tune he knew was Mary Had a Little Lamb.

Hawk tried to get Tommy interested in collecting sock boogers as a hobby instead of music, but Tommy only smiled like he knew a big secret and said, "Trumpets are much cooler than sock boogers."

Hawk didn't know where Tommy got a dumb idea like that.

"You ready to go?" Tommy mumbled. He had half a granola bar in his hand and the other half in his mouth.

"You're not going to take your trumpet to Creepy

Woods, are you?"

Tommy gulped down the mouthful of granola. "How did you know I had my trumpet?"

Hawk pointed to Tommy's backpack. "It's sticking out of your backpack."

"Oh," Tommy said. "I thought I might get bored and want to practice."

"Come in," Hawk said. "I have to get a few things."

They went into the kitchen. Tommy sniffed the air. "Oh, you're having breakfast?"

Tommy most likely had already eaten, but Hawk knew Tommy would eat anything, anytime.

"Good morning, Mr. Kraft," Tommy said. "Good morning, Mrs. Kraft."

"Hello Tommy. Do you want some of my secret breakfast special, dear?" Hawk's mom asked.

"Sure," Tommy said. "I love oatmeal."

Hawk elbowed Tommy in his ribs, hoping he didn't give away the secret that they knew his mom's secret. Hawk watched his mom to see if Tommy's slip of the tongue had registered. There was no reaction. Hawk was relieved.

Hawk had another glass of juice while Tommy ate, then they went to the backyard shed to get the plaster needed to make casts of the tracks.

Hawk's dad said the shed was his workshop, but Hawk had never seen him do any work in it. There were a few tools hanging above the wooden workbench, some screws, and a shelf full of oil that Hawk's dad poured into the family car when it started making noise. There was also a television and an old stuffed chair. On weekends when his mom wanted a lot of chores done, Hawk's dad hid in the shed to watch football and basketball games. He told Hawk when he got older he could hide in the shed with him.

Hawk got the plaster box from a cabinet, and then told Tommy how to use it to make a track mold. "Just mix the powder with water, stir it up, then pour the goop into a track and wait for it to harden into the shape of the track. When it hardens, just lift it out of the dirt."

"Cool beans," Tommy said. "If I poured it on my

face would it make a mask of me?"

Hawk shrugged. "I don't know. We could try it sometime if you want."

Tommy thought about the idea for a few seconds. "Nah. It might stick on my face and never come off."

Chapter 3

The Hole

It was a few minutes after eight o'clock and the sun was bright when they got on their bikes and began peddling towards Creepy Woods. At the last minute, Hawk decided to take Bug Dog along for protection. Bug Dog trotted happily behind their bikes, panting, and occasionally sniffing the road. During the ride, Hawk told Tommy about the meteorite he had seen last night.

"I saw the video on TV last night," Tommy said as they finally reached the park. "Those two old teachers had a really cool fight."

The fight remained the topic of conversation until Hawk stopped his bike at two ancient stone columns that sat on each side of the path at the entrance to Creepy Woods.

Tommy stopped next to him. "Why are we stopping here? Forget something?"

Hawk stared into the park ahead of them. He shook his head. "Nah. Just . . . well, did you ever have a feeling that something bad was going to happen?"

Tommy shrugged. "Sometimes, I guess."

"I have a funny feeling that something important is going to happen today."

"You're creeping me out," Tommy said, looking behind them.

As if agreeing with Tommy, Bug Dog barked, then spun in a circle trying to bite his tail.

RDex stayed in the ship all night. Even though aliens might have seen the crash, he calculated that staying in the ship was safer than wandering around in unknown, and possibly dangerous territory.

When the planet's central star finally rose in the sky, lighting the surface to full brilliance, he decided to venture outside the ship.

The ship wasn't destroyed, but it had been badly damaged in the rough landing. It was almost completely buried in a deep hole it had made on its descent to the planet.

Before leaving the ship and climbing out of the hole, RDex removed the ship's survival kit that had been used by an exploration team many years ago. He set the timer so the ship's invisibility module would activate in five minutes. He hoped the ship had enough reserve power to keep it invisible until he could return to repair whatever damage had been done in the landing. Depending on how the search went for his Primary Guide, it might be a very long time before he was able to return.

Climbing out of the hole was more difficult than he thought it would be. The dirt walls kept crumbling away under his weight. He managed to get out just before the invisibility timers activated and the ship disappeared.

RDex turned in a full circle to inspect the terrain. He was surprised to see so much vegetation. There were small sections in the northern hemisphere of his home planet where scattered patches of vegetation grew, but nothing like the abundance of greenery that spread out before him.

Until he could determine exactly where he was, and if there was any chance of finding his Primary Guide, his safest bet would be to hide in the vegetation in case alien inhabitants showed up. His Primary Guide had sent a video message when she first arrived, so he knew from her report and from the images she had sent that she thought the aliens were peaceful. She had described them as strange-looking creatures with soft bodies covered in self-healing material. Peaceful or not, they looked so ugly that RDex had no desire to meet one.

Chapter 4

Mystery Tracks

Crater Lake, located in the middle of Creepy Woods Park, wasn't really a lake, but more like a pond. Hawk had written a report on the park a few months ago as a geography assignment. While writing the report, he learned that Crater Lake had been formed when a meteorite had smashed into the earth back in the cave man days. He figured it must have rained a lot back then since the hole was now a pond.

Gravel crunched under their tires, and the bright sun warmed their backs as Hawk and Tommy rode their bikes slowly along a trail that cut through the middle of Creepy Woods and eventually led to the sandy shore of Crater Lake. They figured the lake would be a great place for animal tracks since it was the only watering hole for miles.

When they stopped at Crater Lake, Bug Dog

started barking, spinning in circles, and then, without warning, scampered off into the trees.

"What's wrong with him?" Tommy said.

Bug Dog barked only at strangers and Joey Means. Joey was a ninth grade bully who came once a week to mow Hawk's grass. When no one was watching, he gave Hawk nasty knuckle rubs on his head. Hawk's dad said that Bug Dog didn't like Joey because his family owned a bunch of cats. Hawk knew that wasn't the reason.

Hawk whistled for Bug Dog. After a few moments, the small dog emerged from the trees and trotted back to him. Tommy tried to scratch his belly, but the dog was too nervous to lie on his back.

"I think he's afraid of the woods," Tommy said. "Look at his eyes. They look like they're going to pop out of his head."

Hawk sighed. "He's a pug. All pugs have eyes like that. Besides, dogs don't get afraid like kids. He's excited about something. Maybe he smells a wild animal, like a tiger or a wolf."

Tommy moved a step closer to Hawk, looking

around more nervous than Bug Dog.

They decided it would easier to find tracks by walking instead of riding. Tommy was afraid that pirates or teenagers would steal their bikes, so they hid them in a clump of bushes and covered them with leaves.

"I have an idea," Hawk told Tommy. "Let's split up. You go through the trees on the left and I'll go through the bushes on the right. We'll have a better chance of finding tracks."

Tommy didn't like the idea. He mumbled a few excuses, but finally agreed.

Hawk told him to meet him at the lake. Tommy took off toward the trees, looking back over his shoulder until he disappeared into the growth.

Bug Dog followed Hawk with his nose to the ground like dog on a critical mission.

RDex examined the contents of the survival kit. He found an ancient scanner. If it still worked, he could find his Primary Guide with it. He also found a survival module that appeared to be in good working order. He was getting ready to test the scanner when he heard a noise behind him. He quickly stuffed everything back into the kit and hid behind the nearest clump of thick vegetation.

Through the branches he saw three aliens approaching. Two larges ones looked similar to the images his Primary Guide had sent, and a small black alien that walked on four legs instead of two. From the way the small one scuttled about in quick jerky movements, RDex believed it must be their scout, and possibly the most dangerous. He watched the two large aliens dismount their vehicles, and then take separate paths. Rdex was sure they were searching for something, but were they looking for him?

Whatever their intentions, they were headed directly toward the crash site.

Hawk felt a little discouraged. He had been walking for fifteen minutes without seeing a single animal track. He wondered if Tommy had found any.

He paused to listen for Tommy, who was probably no more than a few hundred feet to his right. Hearing nothing, he resumed walking, keeping his eyes on the ground for animal tracks. He was almost to the lakeshore when he heard a noise, a terrible screeching that sounded like a wounded animal in great pain. Another sound quickly followed the first. It had come from Tommy's direction, a horrible noise that ripped a hole in the park silence. Hawk realized his mistake. It wasn't a wounded animal. It wasn't even an animal. It was Tommy playing his trumpet.

Hawk trotted in the direction the sound had come from, wondering why Tommy would be playing his trumpet instead of searching for tracks? He stopped, yelled for Tommy.

A faint voice answered from beyond the line of trees: "Help me!"

Hawk ran through the trees, ignoring small whip-like branches that raked his hands and arms. Past the trees he came to a small clearing.

"Help!" Tommy yelled again.

Hawk didn't see him. "Where are you?"

"Down here," Tommy said.

Directly ahead Hawk saw a hole. It was about ten feet deep and twenty feet across. He ran to the edge and peered in.

Tommy was in the bottom of the dark hole, looking up, holding his trumpet. "What took you so long?" Tommy said.

Hawk took off his backpack, dropped it to the ground. He looked through the pack and found a long piece of rope.

Tommy tossed his trumpet and backpack up. Hawk lay on his stomach and tossed the rope into hole. "Grab the rope," he said.

Tommy grabbed the rope with both hands. Hawk pulled as hard as he could. It took a few minutes and several tries, but Tommy was finally able to climb up the side of the hole, and up over the edge.

They lay on their backs sucking in air. Bug Dog wagged his tail and licked Tommy's face.

"Good thing I had my trumpet," Tommy said, still

gasping. "I might have been in the hole the rest of my life. I played "Mary Had a Little Lamb" so you would know it was me."

Hawk didn't tell him what the screech sounded like.

After they caught their breath, they got up, and slung on their backpacks.

Tommy leaned over to get his trumpet from the ground, and then hesitated. He pointed at a something in the dirt. "Whoa!" he said. "Look at this!"

They got down on their hands and knees for a closer look.

Hawk studied a large depression in the dirt. It was definitely a track, but not an animal track; he didn't think it was human either. Whatever made the tracks had square toes and a round heel.

"What is it?" Tommy asked.

"I don't know," Hawk said, "but the tracks are going that way." He pointed to a line of tracks leading away from the hole and into the bushes. The tracks were very deep impressions in the dirt.

Hawk figured whatever had made them must have been very heavy.

"Let's follow them," Hawk said, trying to sound braver than he felt.

"Uh, why don't we just look around for more tracks," Tommy said.

"These are great tracks. Maybe it's an animal that hasn't been discovered yet. We could be rich and famous."

Tommy looked at his Star Wars wristwatch; one that Hawk knew had been broken for at least three weeks. Tommy snapped his fingers. "Oh, I need to get home. I forgot that I promised my dad I would go to the … to the …er, hardware store with him." Tommy was afraid to follow the tracks, but Hawk understood. He was a little afraid himself, and didn't want to follow the tracks alone.

"We have to get our tracks for Miss Birdie," Hawk said. "Can you come back tomorrow?"

Tommy shrugged. "I guess so."

"Ok, before we go, let's make a plaster cast of one of the tracks. Maybe my dad will know what it is."

Hawk mixed the plaster and, with shaky hands, Tommy poured the goop into the weird track.

Hawk didn't tell Tommy what he thought had made the tracks. He was afraid it would scare him too much. And if Tommy were afraid, he wouldn't come back. Hawk knew one thing for sure: Something very heavy and very strange was walking around in Creepy Woods.

He only hoped it wasn't dangerous.

Rdex was sure the aliens were looking for him. The larger of the two-legged creatures had gone directly to the hole where the ship had landed. At least it was invisible, and unless they had proper equipment, there was little chance they would discover it.

RDex knew he had underestimated the aliens. They were clever enough to quickly locate the crash site. Three aliens would probably bring more so he could not return to the ship, at least not for a long time. In the meantime he would have to rely upon his own wits. He opened the kit, removed the survival module, plugged it into the auxiliary slot in his chest, and twirled the dial to the setting that would give him the best evasion skills.

Chapter 5

Follow The Leader

Hawk woke up on Saturday morning before his eight o'clock wakeup alarm went off. He was anxious to get back to Creepy Woods. He was more interested in the strange tracks they had discovered than in finding animal tracks for his school project. Unfortunately, he didn't get to show his dad the strange plaster cast they had made because his dad had left town on a weekend business trip.

He was sitting at the table eating a bowl of cereal and reading the cereal box when the phone rang. His sister, Wanda, bolted out of the bathroom as if the house was on fire. She was wearing a Justin Bieber bathrobe with a pink towel wrapped around her head. She snatched up the phone before Hawk could reach it.

"Hello," she said, sweetly. After a few seconds, she wrinkled up her nose and shoved the phone at Hawk. "It's your creepy little trumpet friend. Make it quick. I'm expecting a call."

The family used to have a phone in the bathroom, but Hawk's dad had it removed. His dad said that was the only way he could use the bathroom or the phone because Wanda monopolized both. Without the bathroom phone, when Wanda was in the bathroom, she wasn't on the phone. And when she was on the phone, she wasn't in the bathroom. Hawk thought his dad was really smart to have figured that out.

He figured Tommy was calling to chicken out of going to Creepy Woods again. He took the phone from Wanda. It was wet and smelled like perfume. Gross.

Wanda turned around to go back into the bathroom, then stopped suddenly, and screamed. "Mom, help!"

At the same time that Wanda ran out of the bathroom to grab the phone, Hawk had seen his dad sneak into the bathroom carrying a magazine. The combination of his dad and a magazine in the bathroom were deadly and toxic. Hawk's mom called his dad a bathroom terrorist. From experience, even with a full can of room deodorizer, Hawk knew it would be a long time before Wanda would want to go back into the bathroom again.

"What time are you coming over?" he asked Tommy.

"I can't go to Creepy Woods today," Tommy said in a slow, sad voice.

"Why not?"

"I think I might have to do something for my mom today."

"You think you might have to do something? Don't you know?"

The phone went silent for a few seconds. "Well …" he said slowly, "She hasn't asked me yet. But I think she will pretty soon."

Hawk had a plan and knew it was time to set his trap: "OK, I know you're just making excuses. You don't have to go with me if you're afraid."

"Hey, I'm not afraid! I just don't want to make my mom feel bad if she wants me to do something for her."

"Promise on your trumpet that you're not afraid."

Hawk smiled. A trumpet promise was ten times better than a pinky promise. Tommy always told the truth on a trumpet promise because he was afraid it might curse his chances of becoming a famous trumpet player.

An hour later, Tommy and Hawk were on their bikes and headed back to Creepy Woods. They rode directly to the mysterious hole, and climbed off their bikes. Hawk was relieved that the odd looking tracks were still there. Although he hadn't said anything to Tommy, he was afraid that he had only dreamed about them.

They stared into the hole, but couldn't see bottom because it was too dark.

"Don't you think the dirt looks sorta weird?" Tommy said.

"Yeah, it looks black and crusty."

The outside of the hole looked normal, but inside, the dirt looked crusty, black and shiny, as if it had been burned with a flame thrower.

It reminded Hawk of when he and Tommy tried to make chocolate chip cookies. Hawk didn't think his mom would mind if they used the kitchen and her cookie pan. They cut a roll of cookie dough into slices, and then baked them in the oven. They went outside to play and forgot about the cookies until the smoke alarm went off. His mom ran into the kitchen screaming, waving at the black smoke with both hands. When she removed their cookies from the oven, they were black and hard and shiny, just like the inside of the hole.

"Maybe that meteorite you told me about made the hole," Tommy said.

Hawk tried to think of something else that might have scorched the dirt so badly. "Maybe some goofy teenagers built a giant bonfire so they could roast marshmallows."

"Why would they build a bonfire inside a deep hole?"

Tommy had a good point. Something didn't make sense. "If it was a meteorite, then where is it? There's only a hole."

"Maybe it blew up," Tommy said, poking the ground with a stick.

"Everyone in town would have heard an explosion that big. Besides, there aren't any meteorite pieces lying around."

Silence.

"I think you're right," Hawk said. "The meteorite landed here, and then vaporized."

"No way, stuff like that only happens on TV," Tommy said, his voice a little shaky.

Hawk pointed to the strange looking tracks leading away from the hole. "No, it all makes perfect sense now. Everything fits together. Whatever I saw in the sky last night must have landed here. Maybe an alien crawled out of the hole and went into the bushes. We'll be famous if we find it. Miss Birdie will probably give us an A plus on our project."

It took twenty minutes to convince Tommy that

their destiny lay in finding whatever had crawled out of the hole.

Tommy finally agreed to search with Hawk, but only if he could carry his trumpet.

They were back -- the two large aliens and the strange little four-legged scout. They were so close to his hiding place that he could hear them communicating. It had been silly of him to think they had given up pursuing him. He wished there had been a universal translation module in the survival kit so he could understand what they were saying.

RDex wanted desperately to go into hibernation mode and pretend he wasn't stranded on an alien world. Then he could watch his happiest stored memories using the internal viewer his Primary Guide had installed inside of his head.

Of course, he couldn't actually hibernate. Not with the aliens so close. It was only wishful thinking. He couldn't flee either. That would expose his position to the aliens and put him in more jeopardy. There was only one thing left to do. RDex pushed the danger button on the survival module and waited for its expert instructions that would ensure his escape.

The three aliens kept getting closer and closer, and the survival module had not suggested a single evasive action. Maybe it had been damaged in the crash, or more likely, its power source had died a long time ago. RDex rapped on the module with his hand, hoping to jar it back to life. Nothing happened. Desperate, he unscrewed the module from his auxiliary slot and banged it against the ground, then reseated it back into his chest.

Still nothing.

RDex was starting to panic. In a matter of minutes they would see him. He remembered a class lesson taught by one of the ancient explorers, an experienced pioneer who had visited fifty or more alien planets. He had said, " Remember, aliens are just as afraid of you as you are of them."

It had been a good lesson.

RDex decided to put the lesson to a test to see if the ancient one knew what he was talking about.

He checked to see if his courage program was still working, then got ready to confront the aliens.

Hawk noticed that tracks along the trail were irregularly spaced. Some tracks were far apart and some were close together, as if whatever had made them was running at times, and walking at others. The tracks led Tommy and Hawk around the perimeter of the lake and to the other side. When the boys pushed through a row of hedges they found themselves standing in a wide clearing where the tracks had somehow disappeared. Stuck in the ground was a wooden sign with yellow letters that said: PICNIC AREA PLEASE DON'T LITTER.

"That's a great idea," Tommy said enthusiastically. "Let's have a picnic. I packed two sandwiches, some cookies, peanuts, and a big bag of potato chips. Want some?" Without waiting for an answer, Tommy flung his backpack off and began digging through it.

"Not now," Hawk said. "We're on an important scientific mission. We can eat later. The fate of the world might depend on us."

Hawk wondered how the tracks had disappeared? Maybe they had taken a wrong turn. He decided to go back through the hedges to see if he could pick up the trail again.

Behind him, he heard Tommy grumbling, and asked him to stop it.

"I'm not grumbling," Tommy said. "That's my stomach."

Hawk knew Tommy couldn't focus on following the tracks until his empty stomach was filled. Hawk squatted beneath the shade of a small tree and waited while Tommy woofed down a baloney sandwich, a small bag of chips, then guzzled a bottle of orange juice. From the corner of his eye, Hawk noticed the leaves rustling in a large bush about ten feet away from him. Was it a bird? He motioned for Tommy to stop and pointed to the bush.

The bush shook again. The motion was too much to be caused by a bird. Something much larger had moved inside the bush. Then sunlight glinted from something shiny inside the bush.

They watched. After a few seconds, the branches parted.

Chapter 6

Beast in the Bushes

It was an eye. A large, laser-red eye.

Tommy saw the eye, shrieked like a little girl, and started blowing his trumpet in loud, ragged blasts that sounded more like a sick elephant than a musical instrument.

The thing in the bush stood up.

Tommy stopped blowing his trumpet. Both boys froze. Bug Dog seemed disinterested and trotted off to sniff something in the grass.

In the bright sunlight, the creature appeared to be wearing a shiny suit of armor. It stood motionless in the middle of the bush, just staring at them with its round laser eyes.

It reminded Hawk of a skeleton, but instead of bone, it was made of metal. Instead of ribs, the chest and stomach were solid. The surfaces of its arms, legs, hands, and feet were round and smooth with visible joints and gears. It was about the same height as Hawk but appeared much heavier. The thing's head was about the size of a basketball. It had two small holes where its nose should be, and its mouth was a curved piece of metal hinged on both sides of its jaws.

"It's a robot," Hawk whispered to Tommy. When he had first seen the tracks leading from the hole, Hawk immediately thought of a robot. But, at the time, it seemed too fantastic to be possible.

"Wow," Tommy whispered. "It looks like a kid robot. Do you think it is going to hurt us?"

"I don't know. Get ready, but let's wait a second before we run."

For a few minutes Tommy and Hawk stared at the robot, and the robot stared at them. No one moved.

Finally, Hawk said, "I'm going to take a step toward it. I want to see what it does."

"Dude, I wouldn't do that," Tommy cautioned.

"Get ready to run." He stepped forward.

The robot took one step back.

Hawk stepped back, and the robot stepped forward. They repeated the odd dance three more times. Finally, Hawk was convinced it meant them no harm.

"Let's see if it can talk," Hawk said.

"Do you speak robot?" Tommy asked.

Hawk raised his right hand, palm facing the robot. "Hello," he said very slowly.

The robot raised its metal hand the same way. "Hello," it said slowly in a strange mechanical voice.

"Cool," Tommy said.

They were making progress.

Hawk said, "My name is Hawk, what is your name?"

The robot said, "My name is Hawk, what is your name?"

"Oh great," Tommy said. "There's probably a gazillion really neat robots in the universe and we have to find one that's a parrot."

"At least it didn't zap us with a laser gun or some other space weapon," Hawk said.

Tommy snapped his fingers. "I've got an idea." He dug into his backpack and pulled out a package of cookies, and handed them to Hawk. "Give him these."

"Robots don't eat cookies."

"Try it anyway," Tommy said. "It's a kid robot and all kids like cookies."

Hawk shrugged. The cookies were wrapped in foil. Hawk figured a wrapper wouldn't make any difference to a robot, and held it out in front of him. He took a step forward. No reaction. He took two more steps.

The robot remained stationary. When Hawk got within a few feet of it, the robot reached out and gently took the unwrapped package of cookies from his hand. It looked at the package, turned it over, and then shook it. It seemed puzzled by their gift.

"Eat," Tommy said, pretending to shovel food into his mouth with his fingers.

The robot's eyes seemed to grow a brighter red. It ripped the foil wrapper from the cookies, dumped the cookies on the ground, then shoved the foil into its mouth and began to chew.

"Cool beans," Tommy said. "But he wasted the cookies."

The robot held its hand out and said, "Eat."

"He wants more," Hawk said, excited that they had successfully communicated with the robot.

It was almost time to go home. Hawk's parents were expecting them soon. He didn't want to leave the robot stranded in the park, but there was no way to take it home without attracting attention.

"Do you still have your old wagon?" Hawk asked.

Tommy thought for a minute. "Yeah, I think it's in the garage."

Tommy agreed to ride back home and get the wagon. Hawk told him to bring a large blanket, too. Tommy hopped on his bike and pedaled down the trail like he was in an Olympic race.

While Tommy was gone, Hawk asked the robot a few questions. He pointed to the sky and asked him where he was from. He patted his chest and told the robot his name, then asked his.

The robot repeated his questions like a recorder,

but offered no real answers.

Tommy returned thirty minutes later with a beat up red wagon tied behind his bike. A large blue blanket was in the wagon.

"See if he'll sit in the wagon," Hawk said. "Demonstrate so he understands what we want him to do."

Tommy sat in the wagon for a few seconds. He got out and pointed to the wagon, and then pointed to the robot. He did this several times.

"We need to get him in the wagon before someone sees us," Hawk said.

Tommy held one of the robot's arms and Hawk held the other. He didn't resist as they guided him to the wagon, but he would not sit in it.

"What's wrong with him?" Tommy asked, scratching his head.

The robot held out his hand. "Eat."

"Do you have more cookies?" Hawk asked Tommy. "I think he's telling us he won't get in the wagon unless we give him something else to eat."

Tommy kicked the dirt. "Yeah, but I was saving

them for later."

"I'll give you my pirate eye patch if you give him the cookies."

Tommy thought for a minute. He liked to play pirates, but he didn't have an eye patch, and wanted one badly. He always told Hawk it was hard to feel like you're a pirate if you didn't have a patch.

"Deal," Tommy finally said, and pulled the last package of cookies from his backpack.

Hawk felt like Tommy had got the best of the deal. With the patch, Tommy would feel like a pirate, but now without a patch, Hawk wouldn't. He hoped the robot would be worth his pirate patch.

After some difficulty, the robot finally understood. The wheels creaked and the wagon sagged under his weight when he got in. Tommy gave him the cookies. He threw the cookies on the ground again and ate the foil wrapper.

"Wow, he must weigh a ton," Tommy said, studying the bowed wagon.

Bug Dog jumped up in the wagon, licked the robot's hand once.

Hawk covered the robot with the blue blanket, and said, "OK, let's go."

Tommy had a hard time pedaling, so they took turns pulling the wagon. They had to stop three times because the blanket kept blowing off. It took an hour to pull the robot back to Hawk's house.

"Where are we going to hide him?" Tommy asked when they stopped in Hawk's driveway.

"In my dad's workshop in the back yard," Hawk said. "Football season is over, so we don't have to worry about my dad going into the shed to hide."

They didn't want neighbors to see the robot so they untied the wagon from Tommy's bike and pulled it through the side gate and into the shed.

Tommy was breathing hard by the time they got it into the shed.

"What do we do with him now?" Hawk said.

"If he has a switch, we can turn him off," Tommy suggested.

"That's a good idea."

They looked for a switch on his front and back, but didn't find one.

"Robots probably don't get tired," Hawk said. "Just let him stand there until we can figure out what to do with him."

The robot held out his hand. "Eat."

"Wow, he eats more than my dad," Tommy said. "Do you have any more cookies?"

Tommy shook his head. "Nope."

Hawk looked around the shed and got an idea.

A small shelf hung on the wall above his dad's workbench. It was filled with little plastic boxes. Hawk looked through the boxes and found one filled with screws. He poured some screws into the robot's outstretched hand. He popped them into his mouth like he was eating popcorn. When he started crunching the screws, it sounded like someone had dropped a spoon into a garbage disposal.

"Cool beans," Tommy said.

The robot seemed happier after he ate the screws,

"I gotta go," Tommy said. "My parents will get worried if I'm late."

"Me, too. I hope he doesn't get hungry until we

get back."

Tommy and Hawk decided to meet later to make a plan.

Hawk said, "We're either going to be very famous or we're going to be in a whole lot of trouble" Then he added, "Maybe for the rest of our lives."

RDex studied the interior of the enclosure where the aliens had stored him. He was surprised that they lived in such primitive structures. On his planet everyone stored themselves in smooth, clean structures that contained plenty of power sources. This place didn't even have recharging stations or energy pellet dispensers. The floor, the ceiling, and the walls were all made of crudely carved organic fiber slabs.

He had no idea where the aliens had gone, or if they were even coming back. The translation module would have really come in handy. There was a lot of information he needed to extract from them. They might provide some clue as to his

Primary Guide's whereabouts. He remembered the scanner he had salvaged from the survival kit and that he had stored it in a leg compartment. He bent over and popped open the door in the side of his leg and removed the scanner.

But how would he use it? There were no instructions anywhere on the small round disk, and he had never been trained to use one. It should be fairly simple to use once he figured out how to activate it. He had once seen his Primary Guide use a similar scanner to locate another student who had wandered away from the training enclosure after a freak magnetic storm scrambled his memory circuits. He remembered his guide telling him that the scanner, when properly tuned, could precisely pinpoint a distant entity's coordinates, even if they were on the opposite side of the planet.

RDex reasoned that he had two major problems: How did he turn the device on, and then, once it was operating, how did he tune it to his Primary Guide's unique frequencies when he had no idea what her frequencies were. He replaced the scanner in his leg compartment to ponder later. Right now he had another priority. He needed energy. Maybe the odd energy packs the aliens had given him earlier were kept somewhere in this storage facility.

He decided to make a thorough search of the place before his power ran too low for active motion.

Chapter 7

Strangers in the Shed

It was almost dark when Tommy met Hawk in his backyard. There was no light inside the shed. They started to open the door, but stopped when they heard voices inside.

"Do you think your dad found out about the robot?" Tommy whispered.

"No. He was asleep on the couch when I came out."

"Then who's in there?"

They put their ears to the door, hoping they could hear what they were talking about. Most of their words were muffled, but Tommy heard them say something about "stars" and "rockets".

"They're talking about space stuff," Tommy said.

"Maybe aliens came to take back their robot."

"Let's peek in the window," Tommy suggested.

"Maybe we can see something."

There was a small window in the back of the shed. It was too high for Hawk to see inside, so he got on Tommy's shoulders. Tommy staggered around, but finally managed to stand still long enough for Hawk to look in.

"What did you see?" Tommy asked when Hawk slid off his shoulders.

"Nothing," Hawk said. "Just light flickering in the corner."

"Its probably a ninja with a light sword, or maybe the aliens built a portal into another dimension," Tommy said.

Bug Dog was sniffing around their feet. If strangers were in the shed with the robot, Hawk knew Bug Dog would be barking his head off.

They both heard music inside the shed.

"Let's open the door," Hawk said, feeling a little braver with Bug Dog nearby.

"What if aliens are in there?" Tommy said, backing up.

"Then we'll run into the house. I don't think it's

aliens, because Bug Dog acts like everything is OK. The light switch is right by the door. I'll open the door and flip the switch on."

Tommy crouched behind Hawk.

Hawk placed his hand on the knob. "On the count of three, get ready to run."

"I'd sure feel better if I had my trumpet," Tommy said.

Hawk did the countdown, swung open the door, reached inside and hit the light switch. They both jumped back, ready to sprint for the house.

Bug Dog wagged his tail and trotted into the shed. Hawk stepped closer, and looked inside. Tommy had turned and ran halfway to the house.

"Hey, Tommy," Hawk said. "Come here."

Tommy took a few reluctant steps closer. "What is it? Aliens?"

Hawk stepped inside. Tommy peeped through the open doorway.

The robot had his back to them. He had made himself comfortable in the old chair, and had his feet up on a wooden box. The television was on; he was watching a space program on the science fiction channel. In one hand he held a can of oil with a straw in it. The other hand held a small plastic bag filled with screws.

Hawk said, "Hey, that's oil my dad uses for our car."

The robot turned his head. It almost looked like he was smiling. He stuck the straw in his mouth and took a sip of oil. He held up the can and said, "Oil." Then he held up the plastic bag full of screws, and said, "Eat."

"Wow," Tommy said. "He can talk now. Ask him his name."

The robot looked at the TV, then back at Tommy. "We're approaching Saturn, Captain," he said in a deep theatrical voice.

"Huh?" Tommy said.

"He's repeating what he heard on the television," Hawk said. "But since we don't know his name, we should give him one. I discovered him, so how about Hawkbot?"

"That's not fair. I discovered him, too. Why can't

we name him Tommybot?"

"Let's name him something that has both our names," Hawk said. "How about Tomahawk? That sounds cool. The Indians called their hatchets tomahawks, and we both like Indian stuff."

Tommy thought for a minute. "Yeah, Tomahawk. I like that."

A major problem had been solved. Tommy and Hawk slapped high fives.

"Now, the big question," Hawk said. "What are we going to do with him?"

"Can't we just let him stay in the shed?"

"How would you like to spend the rest of your life in a shed?"

Tommy said, "No, but I'm not a robot."

"Tomahawk is a real smart robot," Hawk said. "He seems almost human. He can stay here at night, but he needs to get out, too."

Tommy shrugged. "We can't just let him walk around. People will freak out if they see him."

"You're right," Hawk said, nodding. Hawk was beginning to wish they had never gone to Creepy

Woods. He thought for a minute. Tomahawk was about an inch taller than him, but a little bigger around the waist. That gave him an idea.

Hawk explained his plan to Tommy. At first he wasn't sure if it would work, but the more he thought about it, the better he liked it.

Hawk gave Tommy a list of things he needed. Hawk had his own list of items he would get from his house.

It was getting late. They didn't want their parents to come looking for them. The next day was Sunday so they had all day to work out the details of Hawk's plan.

Hawk was worried about leaving Tomahawk in the shed all night. If he got out and wandered around the neighborhood, he could cause a lot of trouble.

The robot had switched TV channels to a robot show. He picked up a full can of oil from the floor, punched a hole in the top of the can with his finger, and then stuck a straw in the hole.

When one of the robots on television socked

another robot in the face, Tomahawk made a grinding noise that sounded like he was laughing.

Tomorrow they would change him into something completely different.

For the robot's sake, and for theirs, Hawk hoped his plan would work.

Chapter 8

The Big Change

The next afternoon, when Hawk came downstairs, Wanda was sitting on the couch smiling at him like she knew a secret that he didn't.

"Guess what?" she said, chewing her gum.

"I dunno," Hawk said.

"Mom and dad went shopping."

"So?" Hawk didn't know where she was going with the conversation.

"Guess who's *babysitting* her little brother?"

"Come on. Don't say babysitting."

"What wrong with babysitting?"

"Because it's humiliating. I'm not a baby, I'm a grown kid."

Hawk didn't want the kids in his class to know his sister had to baby-sit him.

Wanda crossed her arms over her chest. "What

do you want me to say? Creep sitting?"

"I think kid sitting sounds better," he said.

She laughed. "When you and the little trumpet creep grow up, I'll say kid sitting, until then, get used to it, cause I'm *babysitting* you." She laughed, picked up the phone and punched in a number.

Hawk went in the kitchen but he could still hear Wanda talking to her girlfriend. She kept saying, "babysitting" over and over. He knew she was trying to make him mad, so he went back upstairs, got the bag of things they were going to use on Tomahawk, then went out in the backyard to play ball with Bug Dog and wait for Tommy.

Thirty minutes later Tommy arrived carrying a large paper bag. "I brought everything you wanted."

They went into the shed. Tomahawk was still sitting in the old chair. The television was still on, but it was on a different channel. Tomahawk was watching an old black and white cowboy movie.

"Do you have a camera?" Hawk asked Tommy.

"No, why?"

"I wanted to take a picture because this day will

probably go down in kid history. We're going to change Tomahawk, the robot, into Tomahawk, the kid."

"What should we put on him first?" Tommy asked.

"Clothes," Hawk said, looking at Tomahawk like an artist looking at a painting.

From the paper bag, Tommy pulled out a blue sweatshirt with a doughnut printed on the front, a pair of old jeans with green grass stains on the knees, and a rubber Halloween mask that he had used two years ago. The mask looked like the cowboy on Toy Story. It was the kind that covered your entire head.

Hawk's part of Tomahawk's makeover was a white cowboy hat, brown cowboy boots, and a pair of his mom's white cotton gloves.

"Let's put the jeans and boots on him while he's sitting down," Hawk suggested.

It was hard, but Hawk finally managed to wriggle one of Tomahawk's stiff, metal feet into the jeans while Tommy lifted his leg.

"His leg feels like it weighs a hundred pounds," Tommy said, struggling to hold the leg up. "Maybe more."

"Lift up your leg, Tomahawk," Hawk said, figuring it was worth a try.

Tomahawk looked up from the cowboy movie on TV and said, "Cowboy, have you seen my horse?"

"Forget it," Tommy said, lifting the other leg. "He doesn't know what you're talking about."

They were both sweating when they finally got the jeans and cowboy boots on him. They stood him up, pulled up the jeans, and slipped the sweatshirt over his head. The white gloves slid on his metal hands easily because they were a little big. For the finishing touch, Hawk pulled the rubber mask over his head, and topped it all off with the cowboy hat.

They stood back to admire their work.

"What do you think?" Hawk asked.

"Cowboy, this town ain't big enough for both of us," Tomahawk said.

"I was talking to Tommy."

Tommy walked slowly around Tomahawk, looking him up and down.

"Do you think people will really believe he's a kid?" Tommy asked.

Hawk wondered that, too. A cool kid would never wear clothes like that. "If anyone says anything, we'll think of something to explain why he looks … different. Let's take him out for a test walk. We can see how people react to him. My parents won't be back for a couple of hours."

"What if Wanda sees us coming out of the shed with him?" Tommy said.

"Don't worry. She's always on the phone."

With Tommy on one side, and Hawk on the other they walked him out to the front sidewalk.

"So far, so good," Tommy said.

"No one has seen him, yet."

Before they got to the corner, Hawk saw Mrs. Elders walking toward them. Mrs. Elders had fluffy white hair and glasses so thick they made her eyes look huge. She was a nice lady. When she baked cookies, she always saved a few for Tommy and

Hawk. Hawk's mom told him not to eat the cookies, though. She said Mrs. Elder let her cats lick the mixing bowls and spoons. Hawk always gave his share of cookies to Tommy, who didn't seem to mind the cat taste.

"Hello, boys," Mrs. Elders said. She stopped, peered over her glasses, and pointed her cane at Tomahawk. "Who's your little friend?"

Hawk said, "This is ... er, my cousin."

"That's nice having a cousin," she said. "What's his name?"

"Tomahawk."

Mrs. Elders looked confused. "Tomahawk? Is he an Indian?"

Tommy jumped in. "No," he said. "Tomahawk is from ... er, France."

Hawk wondered how Tommy had come up with the goofy French idea.

Mrs. Elders leaned closer to Tomahawk to get a better look at him. "Well, that certainly is interesting. I think he looks a little like you, Hawk." Tomahawk suddenly blurted out, "Howdy, little lady."

Mrs. Elder's mouth fell open in surprise. "Why, you are such a polite young man," she said. She looked Tomahawk over once more, and then said, "I'd like to stay and chat with you boys, but I have to get home and feed my cats. Stop over later for some cookies. I'll save some for you."

"We will," Tommy said enthusiastically. When Mrs. Elders was a safe distance away he said, "That went great!"

"Yeah, but she's almost blind. We could stand a scarecrow up in front of her and she wouldn't know the difference."

As they were talking, a black car with a bunch of antennas on the roof passed by. It went to the end of the block, turned around and drove by slower than the first time.

"Who are those guys?" Tommy asked pointing to the car as it drove away.

Hawk shrugged. "Dunno. Maybe they were lost. I couldn't see inside the car cause the windows were tinted."

"What do you think about all those antennas on it? You think it might be scientists or the government?"

"Nah," Hawk said. "No one's had time to figure out he landed here."

They had only gone another block when Hawk saw Joey Means on his bicycle, coming out of a driveway about three houses up the street. He was relieved when Joey turned away from them.

"Let's get Tomahawk back to the shed," Hawk said.

"We can stop by Mrs. Elders and get some cookies first."

"No, I think we need to get him back now. I saw Joey Means on his bicycle. He'll be trouble if he sees us."

Tommy didn't like Joey either. Joey was always giving Tommy knuckle nuggies, too.

"Did I hear somebody mention my name?"

Hawk recognized the voice behind him. Joey must have seen them and turned around.

"Hey, Joey," Tommy said weakly.

"Hi, Joey," Hawk said.

"Why are you little creeps sneaking around? Did your mommies let you out to play?" Joey's laugh sounded like a little girl with hiccups.

"Knock it off, Joey," Hawk said, standing in front of Tomahawk.

"Who's your weirdo friend?" Joey said, pointing at Tomahawk. He got off his bike, grabbed Hawk around the neck, and gave him a knuckle nuggie on his head. "How do you like that, Chicken Hawk?"

All Hawk could do was say ouch about a thousand times. He tried to get away but Joey was too big and too strong. Joey was so busy giving Hawk a knuckle nuggie that he didn't notice Tomahawk walking around behind him.

Joey let go of Hawk, and turned to Tommy. "You're next trumpet boy."

Joey took one step toward Tommy. Before he could go any further, Tomahawk said, "Howdy Partner."

Joey started to whirl around, but Tomahawk grabbed the back of his underwear with the best wedgie grip Hawk had ever seen.

Hanging in the air with his arms wind milling, Joey tried to run with feet that didn't touch the ground. "Put me down," he cried. "Ouch! That hurts! Put me down."

"Wedgie! Wedgie! Wedgie!" Tommy and Hawk chanted in unison.

Tomahawk lowered his captive to the ground.

Joey scrambled backward, fell over his bike, and started crying. "I'm going to tell my mommy what you guys did! You're gonna be sorry, real sorry." He jumped on his bike and pedaled furiously down the sidewalk. He was still looking over his shoulder when he disappeared around the corner.

Tommy did a fist pump, and yelled, "Joey is a cry baby!"

"Joey is a creep," Hawk yelled.

Hawk knew Joey was too far away to hear him, but it felt good to yell at him just the same. The next time Joey came over to mow his yard, he didn't think Joey would give him a knuckle nuggie.

Without thinking, Hawk turned to Tomahawk and

lifted his hand in the air. Tomahawk did the same. "High five," Hawk said.

Tommy hooted, and then smacked a high five with Tomahawk like they had been doing it for years.

Chapter 9

Strange Visitor

Mondays were a real drag. Neither Tommy nor Hawk was looking forward to going back to school after the long weekend. They had finished their nature project late Sunday afternoon. After Tomahawk had given Joey a wedgie they had gone back to Creepy Woods and found a rabbit track, a deer track, and a bird track.

While they were waiting for the school bus, Tommy suggested they could get extra credit by turning in the plaster cast they had made of Tomahawk's track. Hawk told him that was a really dumb idea.

Tommy remained silent during the remainder of their wait for the school bus. When they got on the bus, instead of sitting by Hawk, Tommy took a seat in the back.

During the bus ride, their driver, Mr. Rudd, had to stop the bus on the side of the road because Ralph Dinkleton had shoved a spitball up his nose and couldn't get it out. Everyone knew Ralph was one of the smartest kids in school, but they also knew he did a lot of dumb things.

Hawk didn't know what to do as Ralph ran up and down the aisle screaming, "Help me, I'm dying!"

Mr. Rudd seemed not to be bothered about the whole thing. He calmly pulled a red polka dot handkerchief out of his back pocket and told Ralph to put a finger on one side of his nose and blow hard. The spitball shot out of Ralph's nose like a cannon ball and landed in the handkerchief held by Mr. Rudd.

When the ordeal was over, Ralph sat down next to Hawk. He showed Hawk the spitball that had caused all the trouble. "Want to buy it? I'll sell it for a quarter."

"That's stupid," Hawk said.

Ralph looked shocked. "Why?"

"A quarter is too much. I'll give you a dime."

Hawk figured that since Ralph was so smart, he would probably be famous someday. He could save the spitball until Ralph was a grownup, and then sell it on eBay. A rich person would probably pay a lot of money for a spitball that had been stuck up a famous guy's nose. Until then, he could frame it and hang it over his sock booger collection.

"Deal," Ralph said.

They bumped fists

RDex was anxious to begin the search for his guide. If she was in danger, then every moment counted.

At least his time in the storage structure had not been completely wasted. The two aliens had provided what he thought to be a crude, but interesting, language training device. By turning the switch, he could select the training images that most appealed to him. One channel contained realistic images of rockets and beings that looked much like him, and he had mistakenly thought it to be some sort of communicator. He now felt foolish for trying to contact his home planet through the device. Nevertheless, he found himself liking the training device, and looking forward to watching it.

The language gadget had taught him a few of their language phrases, but he had no idea of their meanings, even though he could utter them perfectly. The aliens seemed pleased when he spoke these phrases to them, and because he wanted them to remain friendly to him, he had made a point of saying the phrases as often as possible. Even the ancient alien with white fibers on her head and strange looking eyes seemed very impressed with his command of their phrases.

However, the best thing the aliens had done for him was to provide external skins and coverings that would allow him to move unnoticed among them. If he could only master operation of the scanner, then he could locate and rescue his Primary Guide.

To be sure that he could safely integrate with aliens, he decided it would be necessary to conduct a thorough test of his new skins.

But first, he wanted to find more of those

delicious alien energy pellets and perhaps watch a few more images on the training device.

Miss Birdie began their Monday with a nature film about snakes. The guys thought the snakes were cool, but all the girls were grossed out, except Dee Dawn Steele, who loved snakes more than any other animal. Dee Dawn wanted to be a professional fighter when she grew up and planned to somehow incorporate snakes in her fighting career. On the first day of school, she let Hawk feel the muscle in her arm. Hawk was a bit shocked, not because she let him feel her muscle, but because it was almost as big as his dad's.

At recess, instead of playing tag like they usually did, Tommy and Hawk hung around the swings and talked about Tomahawk. They agreed they should either let him go, or tell someone about him.

"We can't let him go," Hawk concluded. "He doesn't know anything about the earth. Besides, he might get hurt."

"I don't think he could get hurt," Tommy said.

"He's like a superman."

"What about government scientists? They'd probably want to take him apart. I saw some weird looking guys cruising around our neighborhood last night in a black car with a bunch of antennas on it."

"Maybe they're Google guys. I heard they were doing weird stuff."

Hawk shook his head. "Maybe. But one thing is for sure, we can't let him go. It's too dangerous for him."

It seemed like a dilemma with no solution.

"Maybe we could hire Dee Dawn as his body guard," Tommy suggested. Nobody would bother him then for sure."

"She might beat him up if he did something wrong."

The bell rang, and their discussion had to be postponed.

Back in the classroom, Miss Birdie told everyone to get his or her math book out. She wrote three problems on the whiteboard in the front of the room and asked for volunteers to solve them.

A few kids raised their hands. Miss Birdie called on Ralph Dinkleton. As soon as he stood up to go to the board, he started grunting like he had lost the power of speech. Hawk thought Ralph had pulled a muscle or something.

"What's wrong, Ralph?" Miss Birdie asked, rushing over to his desk.

Ralph pointed to the window. "There was a weird looking kid staring at me through the window."

Every head snapped toward the windows, but there was no one outside.

"Maybe you thought you saw someone," Miss Birdie said. "It could have just been a reflection of someone inside the room and it looked like they were outside."

"No," Ralph insisted. "It was a kid. A really weird looking kid."

Dee Dawn raised her hand. "I can go out and kick his butt. Please, please, let me do it, Miss Birdie."

"No, I just want everyone to calm down," Miss Birdie said.

One of the kids in the back of the room shouted, "There he is again."

All heads turned toward the window.

Ralph had been right. Outside the window, a kid had his head against the window, staring into their room.

A chill went up Hawk's back when he saw what the kid was wearing: A cowboy hat and a sweatshirt with a donut on the front. Tomahawk had his face and white gloves pressed against the glass.

Half the class ran to the far corner of the room, shrieking like a bunch of frightened birds.

Tommy covered his eyes with both hands, shook his head, and said, "Oh no."

Hawk put his head on the desk and moaned.

"Settle down, children," Miss Birdie said. "It's just a little boy. I think he's looking for someone. Does anybody know him?"

The class was silent.

Hawk looked at Tommy, who was staring at the top of his desk

Slowly, Hawk raised his hand. "He's … uhh, my

cousin from out of town."

"Hawk, you know we allow visitors from out of town to visit the classroom," Miss Birdie said. "Go outside and invite him in."

"Can Tommy come with me?" he asked.

"Sure," Miss Birdie said.

Once they were outside the classroom and in the hallway, Tommy said, "You should have pretended you didn't know him."

"Miss Birdie might have called the police. Then what?"

Tommy was still grumbling when they led Tomahawk back into the classroom. They stood by Miss Birdie's desk, not sure what to do.

"Introduce your cousin to the class, Hawk," she said, smiling at Tomahawk.

Hawk wondered if he was the first kid in history to introduce an alien robot to his class. "Hi everyone," Hawk said, waving stupidly. "This is my cousin, Tomahawk."

Tomahawk stood motionless, staring at the kids who were all staring at him.

Scott Ratlip raised his hand. "Where's he from?"

"France," Hawk said, quickly. He was glad to have that answer ready. Maybe Tommy wasn't so dumb after all.

"Can he talk?" someone in the back of the room asked.

"He doesn't speak English," Tommy said, and then added, "at least not very good."

Barbie Snodgrass, who wore glasses and never combed her hair, stood up at her desk. "Why is he wearing a mask?"

Hawk was hoping no one would notice Tomahawk was wearing a mask. But there it was: The question he had been dreading. He looked at Tommy, hoping for some help, but Tommy's eyes had gone from looking at the top of his desk to staring at the ceiling. Hawk could feel his face turning red. "Umm ... he has a skin problem," he finally said. "Yes, that's it, he's allergic to American sunlight."

Tommy whispered, "Good thinking. That was close."

"I need to feed my horse," Tomahawk blurted out.

Miss Birdie looked like she was trying to talk, but words didn't come out of her mouth. "Did he say he wanted to feed his horse?"

Hawk said the first thing that popped into his mind. "Like I said, he doesn't speak very good English. He has a cold and he said he feels a little hoarse."

"Oh," Miss Birdie said quietly.

She put Hawk and Tomahawk in the back of the room. Tomahawk sat quietly in the desk for the rest of the class. Tommy and Hawk took him outside with them for afternoon recess. They wanted to play soccer with the other kids, but they also needed to keep an eye on Tomahawk.

"Let him play too," Tommy suggested.

Hawk knew Tomahawk couldn't play, but if he just stood quietly on the field, then they could play with the other kids.

Tomahawk stood in one place and watched the game for about five minutes before a kid on the other team accidentally kicked the ball at him.

What happened next, happened so fast that Hawk didn't realize what Tomahawk had done until it was over.

The other team's goal was at the far end of the playground. When Tomahawk kicked the ball, it became a white bullet streaking across the playground about a foot off the ground; it was still a blur as it tore through the goal's netting, then smashed into the wire fence, where it remained stuck in the dent it had made in the wire.

Exaggerations about Tomahawk's soccer feat spread throughout the school like last year's pig flu. When kids asked Hawk how his cousin had kicked the ball so hard, Hawk was ready with a simple answer. "They play a lot of soccer in France."

By the time the dismissal bell rang at three o'clock, Tomahawk had become a school legend.

Tommy and Hawk secretly high-fived and congratulated each other on being best friends with a legend. They couldn't wait for Tuesday to come so they find out if Tomahawk knew how to play basketball.

RDex was pleased with himself and pleased with his alien friends. His test had gone quite well, and by using the skins and coverings, he had successfully integrated himself into their group.

It was a mystery why the aliens had been so excited when he propelled the sphere across the field with a simple thrust of his foot. He suspected the cluster of aliens scurrying around the white sphere was engaged in an important cultural ritual, and somehow he had accidentally made a significant and meaningful gesture with his foot at exactly the right moment.

RDex felt a special affinity for the alien who he assumed was the guide for the group. Perhaps it was because she reminded him of his own guide. The next time the aliens returned him to their storage unit, he wanted to figure out how to use the scanner.

There was only one thing that really bothered him.

The skin the aliens had put over his head not only made him look grotesque, it also made it difficult to watch the language training machine, and almost impossible to eat the alien energy pellets that he had grown to love.

Chapter 10

The Big Game

On Tuesday morning, Tommy and Hawk decided to let Tomahawk ride the school bus. With Tomahawk in the classroom, they didn't have to worry about him wandering around the neighborhood.

Tommy met Hawk in his driveway ten minutes earlier than normal so they could walk to the bus stop with Tomahawk.

"I'm not sure this is a good idea," Tommy said.

"Don't worry, everything worked out ok yesterday."

Tomahawk was still wearing his cowboy hat and mask. He was dressed in the same blue sweatshirt, stained jeans, cotton gloves, and cowboy boots. In a few days, they would have to change his clothes. While they were waiting for the bus, a black car cruised by.

Tommy said," Isn't that the same car we saw the other day?"

"I don't think so. Don't be so paranoid. There's a lot a black cars in town."

"They don't all have a bunch of antennas on them though."

When the school bus stopped, and the doors opened, Mr. Rudd, the bus driver, gave them a funny look when they got on the bus. "Is he a new student?"

"No," Hawk said. "He's my cousin from France. He's a class guest."

"If you say so." Mr. Rudd shrugged and closed the bus doors.

When the kids on the bus saw Tomahawk get on, they stood up and started clapping and cheering.

They walked down the aisle toward the back of the bus. Hawk turned around to make sure Tomahawk was following and noticed that his mask was twisted sideways. Tomahawk could only see out of one eyehole and the position of the mask made it look like he was looking over his shoulder. Hawk made a quick fix before anyone noticed, and then took a seat in the very back row.

They arrived in class five minutes before the bell rang. Miss Birdie told Tomahawk and Hawk to sit in the back of the class again. Tommy didn't want to be left out, so Miss Birdie let him sit in an empty desk on the other side of Tomahawk.

Miss Birdie seemed happy to see him. "Good morning, Tomahawk," she said, talking very slow. "I'm glad you could join the class again." "Howdy, little lady," Tomahawk said.

He had learned a new trick that Hawk hadn't seen before. Tomahawk tried to tip his hat like he had seen the polite cowboys do on television. But there was a slight problem. Tomahawk tried to lift his hat off his head, but it stuck to his mask like it had been glued on. He tried pulling harder on the hat, but that only caused his rubber mask to stretch into a long, sad face. Tomahawk finally gave up. He released the hat and it snapped back on his head with a loud pop.

Everyone, except Hawk and Tommy, laughed. It took Miss Birdie ten minutes to quiet the classroom. Part of the problem was that Miss Birdie was laughing too.

When it was time for art, Miss Birdie assigned everyone to groups. Hawk, Tommy, Tomahawk, and Mary Lou Taylor were in the same group. They sat around a small circular table.

"Can your cousin draw?" Mary Lou asked.

"I don't know," Hawk said.

"How about toes?" she asked. "Can he draw good toes?"

At the beginning of the school year, Mary Lou announced to the class that she had six toes on her right foot. When they were electing their class president, Mary Lou said if anyone wanted to see her toes, they would have to vote for her. None of the girls were interested in the deal, but most of the guys were eager to see a foot with six toes on it. Hawk and Tommy were both willing to trade their vote for a peek at something that rare.

As things worked out, Mary Lou didn't win the election, and Hawk didn't get to see her toes. Only two guys got to see them, Ralph Dinkleton and Tommy.

Everyone lost interest in her toes when Tommy told them that Mary Lou's sixth toe looked more like a wart than a toe and it had black hair growing out of it. A wart toe was bad enough, but Ralph Dinkleton was so grossed out by the black hair sprouting from the toe, he barfed in Miss Birdie's wastebasket.

Mary Lou asked her question again, but this time she directed it at Tomahawk. "Do you draw good toes?"

After staring at her for about a minute, Tomahawk said, "Oil."

"What did he say?" Mary Lou asked, with a puzzled look.

"That's French," Hawk said. "It means he doesn't draw toes."

"Oh," Mary Lou said, seeming satisfied.

Hawk was glad. The last thing he wanted to see

was her hairy little wart toe.

Having Mary Lou in their group wasn't a total loss, however. She had given Hawk a good idea. It was so obvious; he was surprised he hadn't thought of it earlier.

They might be able to communicate with Tomahawk by drawing pictures.

At recess, it looked like every kid in school was crowded around the basketball court, including several teachers, to see Tomahawk play. Hawk figured Tomahawk should be able to jump high enough to dunk a ball, and with the combination of his computer brain and strength, he could probably sink a shot from the far end of the court, or even from the far end of the playground.

Hawk thought they were going to play kids their own age, but when the other team arrived, it was comprised of three big ninth graders, one of which was Joey Means.

"We're going to ten points, right chicken hawk?" Joey said.

"Yeah, first team to get ten point wins the game," Hawk said.

"We're going to get slaughtered," Tommy whispered.

"Not with Tomahawk on our side," Hawk said confidently.

Hawk won the coin toss. He put Tomahawk under their basket and told him to stay there. Tommy took the ball and passed it to Hawk. Their plan was simple. Every time they got the ball, Hawk would dribble it down court, and then pass it to Tomahawk for an easy score.

Joey Means had his own plan.

As Hawk was dribbling, Joey dipped his shoulder and rammed him. Hawk was slammed backward on his butt. Joey stole the ball and made an easy shot.

The crowd groaned.

"How did you like that, Chicken Hawk?" Joey said, swaggering down court.

"You fouled me," Hawk said. "That shot doesn't count."

"Cheater," Tommy said.

"Tell it to the referee," Joey said, emitting one of his little girl hiccup laughs.

Unfortunately, there were no referees.

With the score 2 to 0, fair or unfair, Hawk and Tommy could either walk off the court or keep on playing, but neither one wanted to give Joey the satisfaction of quitting. Hawk said, "Game on, Joey."

Joey's team scored three more quick baskets running up the score to 8 to 0. Hawk whispered to Tommy, "You were right. We're going to get slaughtered." He gave Tomahawk a hopeful glance, but he still hadn't moved from the spot beneath their basket. Joey's team only needed one more basket to win 10 to nothing. That would be a humiliating defeat.

Joey and his friends were so far ahead they started goofing around and acting stupid. First, Joey dribbled down court with his eyes closed. Hawk ran up behind him, stole the ball and scored. The score stood at 8 to 2.

Tommy also managed to score a basket when Joey threw the ball over his teammate's head — 8 to 4.

Every time Hawk or Tommy scored, the kids cheered.

To save face, Joey tried to put on a dribbling exhibition, bouncing the ball between his legs as he spun in a circle. He lost control of the ball, sending it bouncing into Hawk's waiting hands. Hawk threw the ball to Tommy for another easy basket.

The score was almost tied -- 8 to 6.

Still trying to redeem himself, Joey took the inbound pass for his team. He tried a trick pass to a kid down court, but the ball went out of bounds.

It was Tommy's and Hawk's ball.

Joey called a timeout.

"We've still got a chance to win," Hawk told Tommy as they huddled around Tomahawk, who looked like a lifeless totem pole beneath the basket.

"These guys won't be goofing around anymore," Tommy said. "They're seriously going to kick our butts."

When the game started again, the plan was for Tommy to pass Hawk the ball, and then run as fast as he could to their basket. If Hawk could get the ball to Tommy, he might have a chance to make a basket.

Everything went according to plan. Almost.

Hawk threw the ball high into the air as Tommy ran toward their basket, looking over his shoulder to keep his eye on ball. The ball was still in the air when he ran full-speed into Tomahawk and went down like a piece of limp spaghetti.

Everything seemed to move in slow motion as the ball descended to the court, bounced on Tomahawk's head, and arced into the basket. Swish!

They had tied the game.

Kids went crazy.

Tommy got up, first on his hands and knees, and then to his feet. He shook his head.

"Are you ok?" Hawk asked.

"Yeah, I'm ok. If I had something to eat, I'd feel a lot better."

"Forget about food. Run the same play if we get the ball again," Hawk said. "They won't be expecting us to do it again."

"They'll do anything they can to make the last basket, so watch out for Joey."

Hawk nodded. "I have my own plan for Joey."

With Hawk guarding him, Joey took the ball for the other team and dribbled down court with an angry, determined look on his face. When he got to half court, Hawk pointed to a crowd of kids, and said, "Hey, Joey, is that your mom over there?"

Joey stopped, tucked the ball under his arm, and looked around. "Mom? Where is she?"

Hawk grabbed the ball from beneath Joey's arm. Joey froze in surprise, his mouth hung open like he was sucking in bugs. With their plan in motion, Tommy took off running toward their basket as Hawk threw the ball into the air again. This time Tommy was careful not to run into Tomahawk. But the ball went over his head and dropped into Tomahawk's hands.

Hawk fully expected a spectacular movie-like

ending to the game; he envisioned Tomahawk leaping high into the air to make an amazing dunk.

Instead, Tomahawk just stood there, staring at the ball in his hands.

"Shoot the ball," Tommy pleaded.

The crowd of kids took up the chant: "Shoot, shoot, shoot."

"Give me my ball you French creep!" Joey screamed as he thundered down the basketball court toward Tomahawk. "That's my ball!"

Joey grabbed the ball, but Tomahawk held on. Joey tried twisting it out of Tomahawk's hands. The ball didn't budge. Joey's face turned bright red as he grunted and mumbled strange words. The harder Joey tugged on the ball, the tighter Tomahawk held on. Joey yanked the ball one last time, putting all his strength into the effort.

And then the ball exploded.

Joey screamed like a firecracker had gone off in his pants.

The shredded basketball lay flattened in Tomahawk's hand like a giant piece of limp baloney.

"You cheaters, you popped my basketball," Joey cried. "Now you're really in trouble." He pushed his way through the crowd and ran off.

The bell rang.

Tomahawk's basketball debut had ended in an 8 to 8 tie.

Chapter 11

Family Affair

After school, Hawk and Tommy felt like rock stars as they made their way along the crowded sidewalk that led them to their school bus. They had to maneuver through a gauntlet of high fives, back slaps, and congratulations for the basketball game, and even a few kids who held out pens and papers to be autographed. It was the same on the bus ride home. Even Mr. Rudd wanted to bump fists with Tomahawk.

They got off at their bus stop and went directly to the shed. By drawing pictures, Hawk was sure they would be able to find out where Tomahawk had come from, and why he was on earth. Hawk told Tommy to wait with Tomahawk while he went into the house to look for drawing supplies.

"Hurry up, I have to be home in thirty minutes," Tommy said.

Hawk ran into the house and grabbed a bunch of paper from the computer printer in his dad's office. Then Hawk went upstairs, to get pencils from his desk. His pencils were gone. Two red pencils had been in the desk drawer when Hawk left for school.

He went downstairs into the kitchen. "Mom, have you seen my red pencils?"

His mom was humming a nonsense tune as she stirred something in a pot. "No, I haven't seen them, but check the junk drawer."

The junk drawer was where she put anything she couldn't put in other kitchen drawers. Hawk pulled out the drawer, and riffled through the papers, rubber bands, old batteries, advertisements, and other scraps. No red-pencils.

Benny rode into the kitchen on his tricycle, saying: "Ring, ring, ring."

Hawk noticed he had a red pencil stuck in the back of his pants.

"Hey. That's my pencil," Hawk said.

"Call my number to talk to me," he said, riding around the kitchen table.

"Just give me my pencil."

"No, I'm a cell phone," Benny said. "The pencil is my antenna. Ring, ring, ring."

His mom noticed. "Benny, take that pencil out of your crack. If you fall on it you'll get hurt, dear."

Benny reluctantly withdrew the pencil from the back of his pants and handed it to his mom.

His mom washed the pencil before giving it to him. Hawk was glad.

Tommy was watching a cowboy movie on TV with Tomahawk when Hawk got back to shed,

Hawk spread a few pieces of paper on the workbench. "Let's go, Tommy."

"Wait a minute," Tommy said, pointing at the television. "This is the good part. The sheriff just caught the bad guy."

Tomahawk pointed a finger-gun at the television, and said, "Hands up, you no good cowpoke."

"He's a low down, snake-in-the-grass," Tommy said.

Tomahawk and Tommy slapped high fives.

Hawk noticed that Tomahawk's mask was twisted around again. He tried turning it, but it was caught on a metal stud in Tomahawk's jaw.

"Just take it off," Tommy suggested. "It'll be easier to put it on straight."

Hawk pulled the mask over Tomahawk's head and tossed it on the chair. "We can put it back on after we do the drawings."

"Good idea," Tommy said.

Tomahawk put his cowboy hat back on.

Hawk led Tomahawk over to the bench so he could see the drawings. Hawk wanted to draw something simple first, like his family.

"Let me draw," Tommy said. "I can draw even better than I play the trumpet. I got a C in art last year."

Once Tommy decided to do something, it was almost impossible to talk him out of it. Hawk had seen Tommy's art before. Last month Miss Birdie had given Tommy and Hawk a geography assignment to draw the outline of the United States without looking in their book. Tommy insisted he knew what the outline looked like. When they turned in the assignment, Miss Birdie thought their outline of the US was a picture of a cow.

Tommy picked up the pencil, licked the point, leaned over the paper and began. As he drew, the tip of his tongue flicked back and forth from one corner of his mouth to the other.

"There," he said, looking pleased, "I'm done."

Hawk looked at the three lumpy shapes Tommy had drawn. The two larger figures looked liked mutant cactus, and the smallest one looked like a football with warts. "What are those," Hawk asked.

"That's my mom and dad, and the smallest one is me," he said.

"Let me try," Hawk said. He drew what he thought were reasonably good pictures of his mom, his dad, Bug Dog, and himself. To keep it simple, Hawk left out Benny and Wanda. He slid the paper in front of Tomahawk. "That's me," Hawk said, tapping the drawing first and then himself. He did the same with the rest of the family.

Tomahawk stared at the drawings for a minute,

and then looked at Tommy. He poked Tommy's chest and then touched the paper.

Tommy and Hawk looked at each other and nodded. Tomahawk wanted to know why Tommy wasn't part of the family. He had no way of knowing that Tommy was only a friend. Hawk quickly added a picture of Tommy holding a sandwich in one hand and a trumpet in the other.

Tomahawk made his garbage disposal grinding laugh again, and said, "Tommy eat."

"Is he laughing at me?" Tommy asked.

Before Hawk could answer, Tomahawk picked up the pencil and started drawing on a fresh piece of paper. His hand moved so fast it looked like the picture was magically appearing on the paper. It only took about ten seconds to finish. He drew two robots, a large one and a small one. Both robots looked like black and white photos.

"Wow," Tommy said, "he drew those faster than a robot artist I saw on YouTube."

"He *is* a robot," Hawk said.

"Oh, yeah, I forgot."

Tomahawk pointed to the small robot, and then patted his chest. "RDex," he said.

"RDex?" Hawk said.

"RDex," Tomahawk said, patting his chest.

"His name is RDex," Hawk said.

"Let's keep calling him Tomahawk," Tommy said. "I like that better."

"I think we have to keep calling him that for now." Hawk said, "Everyone thinks his name is Tomahawk. They would think it was weird if we suddenly called him RDex. Besides, I've never heard of a French guy named Rdex."

Tomahawk then pointed to the large robot and said something that had a lot of beeps and tones.

"Parent beans," Tommy said. "If that's his mom, I wonder how you say her name? It sounded kinda spooky with all those whistles and stuff in it."

"We can record it later, then play it back slow. Maybe we'll learn something about his language."

"I wonder if his mom is worried about him?"

Hawk had never given any thought to Tomahawk having a mom, if it was his mom. Somewhere in the universe she was probably searching for him.

"Let's find out if it's his mom or his dad." Hawk pulled out his family drawing again. He pointed to his mom and then pointed to Tomahawk's mom. "Mother."

Tomahawk got a piece of paper from the stack and started drawing again. It only took a few seconds.

The drawing was amazingly detailed. Tomahawk had drawn a picture of every kid in class. They were all standing next to Miss Birdie.

Tomahawk pointed to Miss Birdie, and then pointed to the large robot in his other picture.

"He's crazy," Tommy laughed. "He thinks Miss Birdie is a robot."

"No, I think that's a picture of his teacher." Hawk put his finger on Miss Birdie. "Teacher."

Tomahawk put his finger on the large robot in his picture. "Teacher."

Hawk nodded. He understood what Tomahawk was trying to tell him. "They must not have parents where he comes from. His teacher is probably like a parent."

Tomahawk got up, walked back to the chair, sat down, and stared at the television. A cooking show was on, but he didn't change the TV to the Cowboy Channel like he normally did.

"I think we've made him sad," Hawk said. "Somehow, we have to help him get back to his family."

"Yeah, but how?" Tommy said. "We don't even know where he lives. Even if we did, we don't have a rocket ship."

"Maybe we can figure out a way."

Hawk started to draw a picture of the solar system to find out where Tomahawk had come from when Bug Dog started barking outside. "I wonder who's outside?" he said. "Quick, let's hide these pictures."

Bug Dog's bark had turned frantic.

Tommy froze. "Naked Beans! Tomahawk isn't wearing his mask!"

Before they could move, the door opened.

Chapter 12

Maskless Cowboy

As the shed door slowly squeaked open, light from the afternoon sun spilled around a dark shape that stood motionless in the doorway.

"What are you little creeps doing in here?"

Hawk thought he recognized the voice. "Joey?"

"Yeah, it's me," Joey Means said. "Your worst nightmare."

Tomahawk was sitting in the chair with his back to Joey. From where Joey stood, only the top of Tomahawk's cowboy hat was visible.

"My cousin is in a bad mood today," Hawk said, nodding in Tomahawk's direction. "You'd better leave before he gets mad."

"Your cousin from France? Ok, ok. I didn't know he was in here." Joey took a step back. "Hey, Frenchie, I don't want no trouble, ok? I just came in here to get trash bags for the lawn."

Hawk stepped in front of Joey to block his view of Tomahawk. "The trash bags are in the corner," he said. "Get them and get out."

"What's wrong with Frenchie?" Joey asked, pointing at Tomahawk. "He's just sitting there watching a stupid cooking show. How come he doesn't turn around?"

"Just get the trash bags and leave," Tommy said. "We don't want any trouble either."

"Not so fast," Joey said. "I think you guys are hiding something."

"What could we be hiding?" Hawk said.

Joey snapped his fingers. "That's not really your cousin, is it? That's only a dummy. You must think I'm stupid. You made a dummy to try and scare me, didn't you?"

Tommy and Hawk tried to block his path, but Joey pushed them aside to get to Tomahawk.

Joey skidded to a stop. "What the …?"

Tomahawk turned his unmasked, gleaming metal head and stared at Joey.

Joey's expression changed from anger to surprise, and finally to full-blown horror. He began stuttering.

Hawk knew that Joey would contact every television and radio station in town. Then there would be no place where Tomahawk would be safe from scientists who would dismantle him. Tommy and Hawk would be punished, and probably would never see Tomahawk again. There was only thing to do. Somehow Hawk had to make Joey understand Tomahawk's situation.

Just when Hawk was ready to explain everything, Joey suddenly wilted, falling sideways like a chopped tree. His head bounced on the wooden floor and made a sound like a ripe melon.

"What did you do to him?" Tommy asked.

"Nothing," Hawk said. "I thought you did something."

"Is he dead?"

Hawk knelt down and put a finger under Joey's nose. He felt moving air. "No, he's not dead. He's still breathing. I think he just fainted."

"Sleepy beans," Tommy said, "I've never seen a kid faint before. Can we take a picture of him? Better yet, let's take a video. We could put shaving cream on his face and then put his video on YouTube."

Hawk had to admit that he liked Tommy's idea. But they had more important things to worry about. "No time for that. We need to get Tomahawk out of here."

For the first time, Tomahawk reacted to the sound of his name. He got out of the chair, walked over to where Joey lay, and said in a low, country voice, "He's nothing but a low down, snake-in-the-grass."

"You're right about that," Tommy said.

Tomahawk studied Joey for a few minutes. He made a finger-gun, and put the tip of his finger about an inch away from Joey's head. A small green spark jumped from his fingertip to Joey's temple. Joey twitched a couple of times, and then moaned.

Tomahawk raised the finger-gun to his mouth and pretended to blow smoke from the barrel. He returned to his chair and turned the TV to the Cowboy Channel.

"Get Tomahawk's mask on," Hawk whispered to Tommy. "Maybe it's not too late."

Joey moaned again, sat up, and rubbed his head. "What happened?" he asked.

"You ... er ...slipped. Yeah, that's what happened. You came in here looking for trash bags and slipped on the floor."

Behind Hawk, Tommy snapped the rubber mask over Tomahawk's head.

Joey blinked, looked around, confused. "Where am I?"

"You're in the shed behind my house," Hawk told him.

"How'd I get here?"

"You mean you don't remember?"

"No. The last thing I remember is getting on the school bus this morning."

Hawk had heard of people who were unable to remember anything after hitting their head. It was called amnesia. Hawk helped him up. He staggered, and then stood up. His legs were wobbly.

"You'd better go home and rest," Hawk suggested, steering him toward the door.

"Yeah, I think I will." He opened the door. "Bye Tommy, bye Frenchie. Thanks for helping me."

After Joey closed the door behind him, Tommy did a victory dance. "Dude, that was really close."

"I think Tomahawk wiped out some of his memory. I hope it's permanent. If it isn't and he remembers seeing Tomahawk, then we might be in trouble."

"What can we do?"

Hawk shrugged. "We could always deny it and tell him he dreamed it."

They were relieved that Tomahawk was safe, at least for a while. But, the feeling of relief only lasted a few minutes.

"What's that?" Tommy asked.

"What's what?"

"That noise outside."

Hawk listened. He heard a low whump-whump-

whump.

"You hear it now?" Tommy asked.

"It sounds like it's getting closer," Hawk said, still unsure of what the noise was.

WHUMP-WHUMP-WHUMP

Tommy was talking, but the noise had become so loud that Hawk couldn't hear what he was saying.

"It's right outside the shed," Tommy screamed over the noise.

Hawk cracked opened the shed door a few inches. A blast of air whooshed through the crack, blew open the door, and almost knocked them down.

"Army beans," Tommy said.

Hovering in the sky above the backyard was a large black helicopter. Soldiers with weapons sprouting from backpacks began sliding down ropes dangling from the helicopter.

Chapter 13

Tunnel Rats

When the soldiers hit the ground, Hawk slammed the door and tried to lock it, but there was a slight problem – no lock. Tomahawk was still sitting in the chair, watching a cowboy movie like nothing was wrong.

In a few minutes, the soldiers would burst through the door. Then they would grab Tomahawk and probably put Tommy and him in jail for the rest of their lives, maybe before they could even say goodbye to their parents.

Tommy was frantic. "We need to hide," he screamed.

Unfortunately, the shed was just one small room with no place to hide.

Then a weird thing happened.

Tommy suddenly seemed to grow taller, like he was standing on his tiptoes. "Look," he said, pointing down at the floor. The wooden floor beneath him was bulging up, as if a giant was pushing up on the boards.

"Tall beans," Tommy said, jumping off the hump. "What's going on?"

The boards creaked, shifted, and then began to split apart.

"The soldiers must have dug under the shed," Hawk said.

"Those guys are seriously cool," Tommy said.

Without warning, five or six wooden boards in the floor exploded, exposing a dark hole beneath them. A hand appeared on one side of the hole, and then another hand gripped the other side.

"What's that?" Tommy said.

Out of the hole crawled a ninja dressed in tight black clothes, a black mask, and wearing a small backpack. Without speaking, the ninja quickly removed the backpack, reached inside and took out a small metal cylinder about the size of a Wii remote.

Tommy backed up against the wall, hands out in

front like he was pushing air. "Don't hurt us, please. I'm just a kid. I promise I'll never hide Twinkies in my desk again or sneak Ho-Hos during class movies."

The ninja spun around. "I'm here to help you, not hurt you. We only have a few seconds. Now, quickly, go open the door, take a deep breath and hold it."

Tommy and Hawk froze for a second. The ninja's voice sounded familiar, but there was no time to think about mysteries, so Hawk ran to the door, held his breath, and flung it open.

Two soldiers were only a few steps from the shed when the ninja tossed the shiny cylinder out into the yard. There was a small bang, and then green mist filled the yard and sky. Every soldier stopped running and looked around stupidly.

The ninja slammed the door, and leaned against it. "We have about ten minutes before the gas wears off. The soldiers won't remember anything that happened in the last five or six minutes. If your parents or neighbors heard or saw what was going on, they won't remember either."

"Who are you?" Hawk asked.

The ninja shrugged, pulled off the mask, and shook her hair loose.

Hawk thought he was seeing things. It was a shock he wasn't prepared for. He wondered if he was having a weird dream, the kind he'd had last Thanksgiving after stuffing himself all day with turkey drumsticks and mashed potatoes and cranberry sauce and tons of pumpkin pie.

Tommy looked like he was going to faint. He leaned against the wall for support, then slid down it and sat on the floor. He stuttered a few times, but finally managed to say two words: "Miss Birdie?"

"I'm sorry," Miss Birdie said. "I know this is a shock, but this is an emergency. I'll explain later. Right now, we have to get Tomahawk into the tunnel."

Hawk helped her lead Tomahawk to the hole and down into the tunnel. Miss Birdie had to be the coolest teacher in the world.

"Hawk," she said, "I need your help in the tunnel

to make sure we save Tomahawk."

"I'm ready," Hawk said.

Tommy said, "Do you want me to go first?"

Miss Birdie turned to Tommy and held his face between her black-gloved hands. "No Tommy," she said, "I need you to help in a different way. Do you trust me?"

"Friendly beans," Tommy said. "I trust you, Miss Birdie."

"Thank you, Tommy," she said. "Now, close your eyes."

From a pocket on her ninja suit, Miss Birdie removed a small black tube, and sprayed Tommy in the face.

Tommy blinked a few times, and said, "I ... I ... feel ... kinda ... weird."

"Listen to me, Tommy," she said. "After we go down the tunnel, I want you to put the rug and chair over the hole. You won't remember that Tomahawk, Hawk, or I were here. After you cover the hole, then sit in the chair and watch television. If anyone comes in, say you were just watching TV and waiting for Hawk. Do you understand?"

Tommy blinked again. "I ... understand ... Miss ... Birdie."

Once in the tunnel, they heard Tommy sliding the furniture across the floor above them.

The tunnel was tall enough for Hawk to walk through without bending over, but it was also dark and hard to see where he was going.

Miss Birdie whispered something to Tomahawk, and a little panel slid open in his forehead. Behind the panel, a bright spotlight came on, illuminating the tunnel ahead of them.

Hawk had a lot of questions. He didn't understand how Miss Birdie knew about the soldiers or how she could have dug such a large tunnel so fast or how she knew what to say to Tomahawk to make the light come on. When Hawk asked her about it, all she said was "Later."

They had gone about one hundred yards, when Hawk noticed something strange. About halfway up the tunnel wall, a small door had been exposed in the dirt wall. The door had yellow metal hinges, and looked much like the door on a large safe. He wanted to stop to investigate for a few minutes.

"We can't stop," Miss Birdie said. "We only have a short distance to go, and we have very little time left."

Hawk's curiosity was killing him. "What is a door doing underground?"

"I don't know, Hawk," she said. "When I was on my way to help you in the shed, I detected a very strong magnetic field in this area. When everything is normal again, you can come back and investigate. But not now."

Without another word, Miss Birdie spun around and resumed walking toward the other end of the tunnel,

As Hawk followed behind her, he wondered if his life would ever be normal again.

Chapter 14
A New Kid

Hawk stepped out of the tunnel and into the cool night air. They were behind a bush in a neighborhood playground not far from his house.

Miss Birdie pointed across the street. "That's my car over there. We need to make sure no headlights are coming, then we'll walk Tomahawk to the car."

Where are we going?" Hawk asked.

"My house," she said. "Everything that I need is there."

Hawk wondered what she meant by "everything" and why she needed "everything."

After a thirty-minute drive during which no one spoke, Miss Birdie pulled the car into her garage. The garage door rolled down behind them. Tomahawk and Hawk followed Miss Birdie into the house, where they passed through a small kitchen with white curtains and stopped at a door in the hallway. Miss Birdie opened the door, revealing a stairway that led down to the basement.

In the basement, Miss Birdie used her finger to trace a complicated pattern next to a light switch on the basement wall.

Hawk heard a whirring noise, then a hidden door slid open revealing a large room beyond that was filled with electronic gadgets, a long bench lined with strange shiny tools, and a row of large metal cabinets. A narrow table on wheels sat in the middle of the room. Above the table, several adjustable spotlights hung from the ceiling.

Hawk had seen doctor shows on television and knew it was an operating room. He trusted Miss Birdie, but the operating table scared him. "Miss Birdie, can you tell me what's going on?"

Miss Birdie picked up a tool that looked like a twisted screwdriver, then put it down, and turned to face him. "Are you sure you want to know, Hawk? You might find out things you really don't want to know."

Hawk shook his head. "No, tell me. Please."

She thought for a minute, and then sighed. "Ok, I guess we have time now. But remember, you wanted to know."

"Let's start with this first." Miss Birdie grabbed a handful of her hair and pulled up hard. Her face stretched slowly into a long thin expression like Tomahawk's had done when his rubber mask had stuck to his cowboy hat. Miss Birdie's face finally popped off.

Seeing Miss Birdie as a ninja had been incredible enough, but the sight of the new Miss Birdie sent a jolt of disbelief through Hawk. For a moment he felt dizzy, and wondered if he was trapped in a bizarre dream that would end when he woke up in his own bed with Bug Dog licking his face.

At that moment, all he could do was mumble: "You ... you ... you're a robot?"

With her mask off, and her real countenance revealed, Miss Birdie looked much like Tomahawk, except that her bright metallic head was smoother and rounder than his. She still wore her blue human eyes and eyelashes, which were a strange contrast to her robot features.

Tomahawk seemed as surprised as Hawk. He stared at her for a few seconds. Suddenly he raised both arms in the air like he was trying to catch a fly ball and rushed to Miss Birdie. Tones and beeps and pulses started to flow between them, slowly at first, and then faster and faster, until the individual sounds blended into a single braided tone. For several minutes, the tangle of unearthly sounds seemed to fill the small room as they echoed off the hard concrete walls.

It was clear to Hawk that Tomahawk was happy, probably for the first time since he had encountered his robot friend in Creepy Woods.

After a few minutes, the strange sounds ceased. Miss Birdie retrieved her mask from the table, pulled it back on, and then turned to face Hawk.

"I explained everything to RDex," she said. "I recognized him the minute you brought him into the classroom. I couldn't believe he was here. I suspected he had run away, so that's when I started preparing all this for him."

She went to the wall near the door and pressed her hand against a black plate. A contraption that looked like a large bed with a hinged lid slid out of the wall. Attached to the lid were four transparent hoses and a row of gauges and buttons. The other ends of the hoses were attached to large tanks inside the wall.

Miss Birdie opened the lid. The bottom part of the bed looked like a kid had fallen into a large piece of clay with his arms and legs spread out. "We're going to make a few changes to RDex," she said. "But first I need to install something."

She touched her head to Tomahawk's and emitted a series of high and low beeping sounds. Tomahawk beeped back, and then removed his cowboy clothes, white gloves, and cowboy hat. He sat down in the chair next to the slide-out bed. Miss Birdie went to the cabinets, opened a drawer and pulled out a tool resembling a miniature hockey stick. From another drawer she removed a shiny blue disk. She squeezed the disk between two fingers and a row of green lights lit up around its edge.

"This is a translation module," she said holding up the disk. "Once I install it, RDex will be able to understand and speak any language on earth."

"You couldn't put one of those in me, could you?"

Miss Birdie smiled. "I'm afraid not, Hawk."

Using the miniature hockey stick tool, she opened a flap in Tomahawk's side and inserted the flashing blue disk. After she closed and locked the flap, Tomahawk stood up, climbed into the bed, and fitted his arms and legs into the pre-made depressions.

Miss Birdie closed the lid and adjusted a few dials.

Hawk watched as green liquid started flowing through two of the clear hoses and yellow liquid ran through the other two.

"The transformation will take about ten minutes,"

Miss Birdie said.

While they waited she told Hawk the rest of her story.

"I was a scientist on my planet. My job was to train young robots how to manufacture other robots. When an exploration team visited to your solar system they discovered your race. You have to understand that humans were something totally amazing to us. You didn't need factories to build other people. Your body repaired itself whenever you got hurt. Your body grew from young to old without needing anyone to install new parts for the process.

"My planet sent me here to find out how humans did that. That's why I got a job in your school as a teacher. What better way to learn about growth than to be around young humans?"

A bell rang on the machine behind her.

"RDex is ready to be taken out of the molding transformer," Miss Birdie said. She pushed a few more buttons, and then lifted the lid.

Tomahawk lay inside the machine, but he no

longer looked like he was made of metal and gears. The rubber-molding machine had changed him into a regular looking kid with dark brown hair and tan skin. He opened his eyes, blinked, and then sat up. He stretched his arms and flexed his fingers, then climbed out of the machine, and began dressing himself in Tomahawk's old clothing.

"Hawk," Miss Birdie said, "meet my new nephew, and your new friend and classmate, Robert Dexter, from France."

Hawk was so stunned he could not move or speak. Finally he managed to utter one word: "Wow!"

The new Robert Dexter, the old Tomahawk/RDex, stuck out his hand. Hawk weakly shook hands with him.

Robert opened his mouth to speak, but emitted only a few squeaks. He turned to Miss Birdie and looked at her as if asking her what was wrong with him.

"Keep trying," she encouraged. "It takes the translator module a few minutes to synchronize."

Robert emitted a few more beeps, and then a few words came out but they were slow and stretched out, like the sound in a slow motion movie scene. The words gradually sped up until they sounded like perfect English. "Wow," he finally said, "it's really weird to talk like this."

Hawk started to ask him a question, but Miss Birdie stopped him.

"We can chat later," she said. "We need to get back to your house before people start asking questions."

On the ride back to Hawk's house, RDex sat in the front seat while Hawk sat in the back. RDex stared at his new hands. His Primary Guide had given him the ultimate disguise. With his new skin covering and power of speech, he would be able to stay on this planet until her assignment was complete. She had already sent a communication back to the elders of his planet to let them know he had arrived safely. They told her that his punishment would be decided when they returned.

At least he now knew his Primary Guide was safe, although he hoped he could get used to her appearance and to calling her by her strange alien name, Aunt Birdie. He would also have to get use to his new alien name.

He had grown fond of this planet and of his two alien friends. He would be sad to leave them when his time for departure came, but he would especially sorry to leave the delicious and crunchy alien power pellets.

When they arrived in Hawk's backyard, the skies were clear, no helicopters or soldiers were in sight. Inside the shed, the television blared with the sound of cowboy gunshots. Tommy was curled in the chair asleep.

Miss Birdie smiled. "I'll bet there are some very embarrassed soldiers somewhere in town who are explaining to their general why they staged a massive helicopter raid on a little boy watching cowboy movies in a backyard shed."

Robert stared at the television. "Can I come back

and watch cowboy movies with Hawk sometime?"

"Of course you can," Miss Birdie said. "Hawk, you'd better wake up Tommy."

Hawk shook Tommy by his shoulder. "Wake up. It's time to go home."

Tommy blinked his eyes, stretched, and yawned. "Where did you guys go? Where's Tomahawk?"

"Who's Tomahawk?" Miss Birdie asked.

"You know, the rob … er … I mean, our friend."

"You must have been dreaming," Hawk said.

Tommy looked confused. He scratched his head. "It seemed so real."

"Just kidding," Hawk said. "I'll tell you everything later."

Miss Birdie stepped forward. "Tommy I want you to meet my nephew."

Robert stepped forward. "Hi, my name's Robert. I've heard a lot about you from Aunt Birdie."

Tommy bumped fists with Robert. "Cool Beans."

"I need to talk to Hawk's parents and make sure everything is ok," Miss Birdie said, "Why don't the three of you get acquainted while I'm gone?"

"I have something we can do," Hawk said. "We'll be in later."

Miss Birdie winked at Hawk, then left the shed.

When the door closed behind her, Hawk went to the workbench and began frantically opening and closing drawers.

"What are you doing?" Tommy asked.

"Looking for a flashlight." He opened the bottom drawer and found what he was looking for.

"Why do you need a flashlight?" Tommy said.

"We need it for this." Hawk went to the middle of the shed, moved the chair, and pulled back the rug, exposing the rescue tunnel entrance Miss Birdie had made. "Follow me."

"I've never seen that before," Tommy said.

Hawk dropped into the tunnel, followed by Robert, then Tommy.

Hawk didn't stop until he reached the exposed small metal door he had seen during their escape from the soldiers. He gave the flashlight to Tommy and told him to shine it on the door. Hawk grasped the handle with both hands and twisted, but it didn't budge. He tried again, exerting all his strength, but the handle remained stuck.

"Let me try," Robert said. He put one hand on the handle, twisted effortlessly, and the door popped opened.

"Strong Beans," Tommy said. "What's inside, Hawk?"

Hawk took the flashlight, looked inside the door and realized he didn't need a flashlight. Daylight spilled out of the door and lit up the tunnel. The scene inside the door seemed like a magnet that would not release his eyes. It was a scene right out of a science fiction movie.

"What's in there?" Tommy said.

Hawk closed the door, and then turned to face them. "I think we've found our next adventure," he said. He needed a few minutes to digest what he had seen. The door was a portal into another an expansive world, perhaps even another dimension, but most surely another time.

In the distance, far beyond the door, he'd seen something almost too incredible and too amazing to be real. Standing majestically in a distant lake, surrounded by giant ferns and tall trees, he was sure he had seen a herd of grazing brontosaurus and at least one ferocious looking T-Rex.

THE END

Dear Reader,

Thank you for joining us on this adventure with Tommy and Hawk. We have enjoyed creating these characters and we hope you enjoyed reading about them.

Books allow you to fly as far your imagination will take you. We urge you to read as much as you can. It will expand your horizons and help you be creative and successful in all your life endeavors.

We invite you to join us in the next book, **Runaway Alien: Time Tunnel**, when Tommy, Hawk, and Robert (Tomahawk) explore an adventure-filled world of smart dinosaurs, invisible animals, stranded aliens, and where the evil leader of cave people will stop at nothing to capture them.

Visit us at www.runawayalien.com for more information. We would love to hear your comments about the book. Our email address is robot@runawayalien.com.

Alec Eberts and Paul Smith-Goodson

ABOUT THE AUTHORS

Alec and his grandfather, Paul, started Runaway Alien when Alec was in the third grade. During the summer, they finished most of the book, but the project was delayed for a few months for lack of a good ending. They finally published an electronic ebook version of the book in January 2012 and a paperback in February of that year.

Alec is currently in the fourth grade. He likes reading, golf, soccer, basketball, and football. He also enjoys online games, especially Wizard 101 and Free Realms.

Alec's grandfather, Paul, has been retired from the corporate world for a number of years. He has been married to Alec's grandmother, Joan, for 46 years. In addition to Alec, they have nine other grandchildren.

22895760R00083

Made in the USA
Lexingtón, KY
18 May 2013